The Tale of
Mr. Peter Brown

The Tale of
Mr. Peter Brown
V. Sackville-West

MINT EDITIONS

The Tale of Mr. Peter Brown was first published in 1900.

This edition published by Mint Editions 2021.

ISBN 9781513212159 | E-ISBN 9781513212050

Published by Mint Editions®

 MINT
EDITIONS

minteditionbooks.com

Publishing Director: Jennifer Newens
Design & Production: Rachel Lopez Metzger
Project Manager: Micaela Clark
Typesetting: Westchester Publishing Services

The first thing which attracted my attention to the man was the shock of white hair above the lean young face. But for this, I should not have looked twice at him: long, spare, and stooping, a shabby figure, he crouched over a cup of coffee in a corner of the dingy restaurant, at fretful enmity with the world; typical, I should have said, of the furtive London nondescript. But that white hair startled me; it gleamed out, unnaturally cleanly in those not overclean surroundings, and although I had propped my book up against the water-bottle at my own table, where I sat over my solitary dinner, I found my eyes straying from the printed page to the human face which gave the promise of greater interest. Before very long he became conscious of my glances, and returned them when he thought I was not observing him. Inevitably, however, the moment came when our eyes met. We both looked away as though taken in fault, but when, having finished his coffee and laid out the coppers in payment on his table, he rose to make his way out between the tables, he let his gaze dwell on me as he passed; let it dwell on me quite perceptibly, quite definitely, with an air of curious speculation, a hesitation, almost an appeal, and I thought he was about to speak, but instead of that he crushed his hat, an old black wideawake, down over his strange white hair, and hurrying resolutely on towards the swing-doors of the restaurant, he passed out and was lost in the London night.

I was uncomfortably haunted, after that evening, by a sense of guilt. I was quite certain, with unjustifiable certainty born of instinct, that the man had wanted to speak to me, and that the smallest response on my part would have encouraged him to do so. Why hadn't I given the response? A smile would have sufficed; a smile wasn't much to demand by one human being of another. I thought it very pitiable that the conventions of our social system should persuade one to withhold so small a thing from a fellow-creature who, perhaps, stood in need of it. That smile, which I might have given, but had withheld, became for me a sort of symbol. I grew superstitious about it; built up around it all kinds of extravagant ideas; pictured to myself the splash of a body into the river; and then, recovering my sense of proportion, told myself that one really couldn't go about London smiling at people. Yet I didn't get the man's face out of my head. It was not only the white hair that had made an impression on my mind, but the unhappy eyes, the timidly beseeching look. The man was lonely, I was quite sure of that; utterly lonely. And I had refused a smile.

I don't know whether to say with more pride than shame, or more shame than pride, that I went back to the restaurant a week later. I had been kept late at my work, and there were few diners; but he was there, sitting at the same table, hunched up as before over a cup of coffee. Did the man live on coffee? He was thin enough, in all conscience, rather like a long, sallow bird, with a snowy crest. And he had no occupation, no book to read; nothing better to do than to bend his long curves over the little table and to stab at the sugar in his coffee with his spoon. He glanced up when I came in, casually, at the small stir I made; then by his suddenly startled look I saw that he had recognised me. I didn't nod to him, but I returned his look so steadily that it amounted to a greeting. You know those moments, when understanding flickers between people? Well, that was one of those moments.

I sat down at a table, placing myself so that I should face him, and very ostentatiously I took a newspaper out of my pocket, unfolded it, and began to read. But through my reading I was aware of him, and I knew that he was aware of me. At the same time I couldn't help being touched by what I knew I should read in his face: the same hostility, towards the world at large, and towards myself the same appeal, half fearful, half beseeching. It was as though he said, aloud and distinctly, "Let me talk! For God's sake let me talk it out!" And this time I was determined that he should; yes, I was quite grim over my determination. I was going to get at the secret that lay behind those hunted eyes.

I was in a queer mood myself; rather a cruel mood, although the starting-point of my intention had been kind. I knew that my mood had something of cruelty in it, because I discovered that I was purposely dawdling over my dinner, in order to keep the man longer than necessary on the rack. Queer, the complexities one unearths in oneself. But probably if I had been an ordinary straightforward kind of fellow, I should never have had the sensibility to recognise in the first instance that the man wanted to talk to me. It's the reverse of the medal, I suppose.

He had finished his coffee, of course, long before I had finished my dinner; he had squeezed the last drop out of the little coffee-pot, and I wondered with amusement whether he would have the moral courage to remain where he was now that his ostensible pretext was gone and that the waiter was beginning to loiter round his table as a hint that he ought to go. Poor devil, I could see that he was growing uneasy; he shuffled his feet, and the glances he threw at me became yet more furtive and reproachful. Still I gave no sign; I don't know what spirit of sarcasm and teasing possessed me. He stood it for sometime, then he shoved back his chair, reached for his hat, and stood up. It was a sort of defiance that he was throwing at me, an ultimatum that I should either end my cat-and-mouse game, or let him go. As he was about to pass my table on the way out, I spoke to him.

"Care for a look at the evening paper?"

Absurd—isn't it?—that one should have to cloak one's interest in a stranger's soul under such a convention as the offer of a paper. Why couldn't I have said to him straight out, "Look here, what's the matter with you?" But our affairs are not so conducted. He accepted my offer, and stood awkwardly reading the *City News*, which I thought a sure indication of his confusion, as by no stretch of fancy could I imagine him the possessor of stocks or shares. "Sit down," I said, "while you read."

He sat down, with a mumble of thanks, laying his old black wideawake beside him on my table. I think he was glad of the paper, for it gave him something to do with his hands and his eyes. I observed him, and he must have known I was observing him. Underneath the thick, snow-white hair the face was young, although so sunken and so sallow, the face of a man of perhaps twenty-seven or eight, sensitive, not at all the face of a criminal escaping from justice, in spite of that hunted look which had been so vividly present to me during the past week. An artist, I thought; perhaps a writer; a romantic face; not blatantly romantic; no, but after you had delved into the eyes and traced the quiver of the mouth you discovered the certain signs of the romantic idealist.

"I saw you here last week," he muttered suddenly.

The little restaurant was by now almost empty; many of the lights had been turned down, and at most of the tables the chairs had been tipped forward. Being privileged as an old and regular customer, I beckoned to the proprietor, and in a whisper begged that I might not be disturbed, as I had to hold a business conversation of some importance with my companion. At the same time I poured out for the stranger a glass of wine from my own bottle, remarking that the wine here was better than their coffee. This seemed to unloose his tongue a little, for he exclaimed that coffee was very bad for the nerves, especially strong, black coffee, as he drank it; and after this short outburst relapsed again into silence, taking refuge in the paper.

I tried him once more.

"I don't remember seeing you here before last week?"

He shot me a quick look, and said, "I haven't been in London."

"Travelling, perhaps?" I hazarded negligently.

He gave a harsh shout of laughter, succeeded by the same abrupt silence. Would all our conversation, I wondered, be conducted on this spasmodic system? He certainly didn't second my efforts at small-talk. Was what he had to say too vital, too oppressive?

"I say," I resumed, leaning forward, "have I seen you anywhere else? I think your face is familiar. . ." It was a lie; I knew perfectly well that I had never seen him anywhere; his was not an appearance to be lightly forgotten.

"And yet," I added, as he stared at me without speaking, "I am sure I should remember; one would remember this contrast"—and I touched first my face and then my hair.

"It has only been like that for a fortnight."

He brought out the words, scowling and lowering at me, and then the fierce look died away, to be replaced by a look of apology and pain; a cowed look, like that of a dog who has been ill-treated. "That is what made you notice me," he exclaimed; "it brands me, doesn't it? Yes. A freak. One might as well be piebald." He spoke with extraordinary vehemence, and, taking a handful of his hair, he tugged at it in a rage of despair; then sinking his face between his hands, he sat shaking his head mournfully from side to side.

"Listen," I said, "have you any friends?"

He raised his head.

"I had a few stray acquaintances. Nothing would tempt me to go near them now."

"Anyone to talk to?"

"Not a soul. I haven't spoken to a soul since—since I came back."

"Fire ahead, then," I said, "talk to me. You don't know my name, I don't know yours. You're quite safe. Say whatever you like. Go on. I'm waiting."

He began, talking in a voice low, rapid, and restrained. He spoke so fluently that I knew he must often have rehearsed the phrases over to himself, muttering them, against the day when he should be granted expression. "I had two friends. They were very good to me. I was homeless, and they told me to look on their home as my own. I hope I didn't trespass too much on their hospitality, but I fell into the habit of wandering into their house every evening after dinner, and staying there till it was time to go to bed. I really don't know which I cared for most, in those early days, the man or the woman. It had been with him that I first made acquaintance; we were both engaged on journalistic work, reporting, you know, on different papers—and we came across each other once or twice in that way. He was a saturnine, queer-tempered fellow, taciturn at times, and at other times possessed by a wry sense of humour which made him excellent company, though it kept one in a state of alert disquiet. He would say things with that particular twist to them which made one look up, startled, wondering whether his remark was really intended to be facetious or obscurely sinister. Thanks to this ambiguity he had gained quite a reputation in Fleet Street. You can imagine, therefore, that I was flattered when he singled me out; I listened to all his remarks with a respect I was too proud to betray; although I adopted an off-hand manner towards him, I didn't lose many opportunities of letting the other fellows know, in a casual way, that I had been practically given the run of his house; and I was never sorry to be seen when we strolled off with his arm in mine.

"They lived, he and his wife, in a tiny house at the end of Cheyne Walk. On misty evenings we used to sit, all three, on the sill of the bow-window, watching the big barges float by, while our legs swung dangling from the high sill, and we talked of many things in the desultory way born of easy intimacy, and I used silently to marvel at the sharpness of his mind and the gentleness of hers. She was very gentle. It even irritated me, faintly, to observe her complete submission to him. Not that he bullied her, not exactly. But he had a way of taking submission for granted, and so, I suppose, most people accorded it to him. It irritated me to see how his wife had subdued her personality to his, she who was of so tender and delicate a fibre, and who more than anyone wanted cherishing, instead of being ridden down, in that debonair, rough-shod way of his, that, although often exasperating, still had something attractive about it. She and I used to discuss it sometimes, in the evenings, when he was kept out late at his job—it's an uncertain business, reporting—we used to discuss it with the tolerance of fond people, and smile over his weaknesses, and say that he was incorrigible. All the same, it continued to irritate me. Sometimes I could see that he hurt her, when in his impatient way he swung round to devastate her opinions with those sly and unanswerable phrases that placed everything once and for always in a ridiculous light. What a devilish gift he had, that man, of humiliating one! And he did it always in so smiling and friendly a fashion that one could neither take offence nor retaliate. In fact, one didn't realise that one had been attacked until one felt the blood running warm from one's wounds, while he had already danced away upon someother quest.

"I can hardly trace the steps by which my admiration of him grew to affection, my affection to uneasiness, and my uneasiness to resentment. I only know that I took to flushing scarlet when I saw her wince, and to making about him, when I was alone with her, remarks that were less and less tolerant and more and more critical. My temper grew readier to bite out at him, my amusement less easily beguiled. I don't know whether he noticed it. Most probably he did, for he always noticed everything. If he did, then he gave no sign. His friendliness towards me continued unvarying, and there were times when I thought he really bestirred himself to impress me, to seduce me, he who was usually so contemptuous, and seemed to enjoy stirring up people's dislike. It wasn't difficult for him to impress me, if that was what he wanted, for he had, of course, a far better brain than my own; the sort of brain that compelled one's startled admiration, even when one least wanted to accord it. By Jove, how well he used to talk, on those evenings, when we sat and dangled our legs from the window-sill, looking out at the barges! The best talk I ever heard. You could have taken it all down in shorthand, and not a word to alter.

"Then he got a regular job which kept him out for three evenings a week, but he told me that mustn't make any difference to my habits: I was to drop in just the same, whenever I wanted to; and since I hadn't anywhere else to go, and since the house had become a home to me, I took him at his word. In a way I missed him, on the evenings he wasn't there; although I could no longer pretend to myself that I was fond of him, he was a perpetual interest and stimulation to me, an angry stimulation, if you can understand what I mean, and I missed his presence, if only because it deprived me of the occupation of picking holes in him, and of making mental pounces for my own satisfaction upon everything he said. Not upon its intellectual value. That was above reproach. Only upon it as a signpost to his character. I took a delight in silently finding fault with him. But presently this desire passed from me, and I came to prefer the repose of the evenings I spent alone with his wife to the strenuousness of the evenings when we were all three together. We talked very little, his wife and I, when he was not there. She had about her an amazing quality of restfulness, of which I quickly got into the habit of taking advantage, after the vulgar, competitive days of a journalist's existence. You can't imagine what it meant to me, to drift into the seclusion of that little Chelsea room, with the mistiness of the trees and the river outside the window, to be greeted by her smile, and to sink into my familiar arm-chair, where I might lounge sucking at my pipe and watching the cool glimmer of her beautiful hands over the rhythm of her needle. Can you wonder that we didn't talk much? And can you wonder that our silence became heavy with the things we hadn't said?

"Not at first. Our love-affair ran a course contrary to the usual ordering of such things. If it indeed ended in all the fever and pain of passion, it certainly began with all the calm of the hearth; yes, I went through a long phase of accepting that room as my home, and that gentle woman as my natural companion therein. I don't think I examined the situation at all closely at that time. I was more than content to let so pleasant an acquiescence take possession of me; for the first time in my life, you understand, I was neither lonely nor unhappy. The only thing that jarred was *his* presence. The evenings when *he* was there were all out of tune. All out of tune."

The man with the white hair paused to pour himself out another glass of wine; and his voice, losing the dreamy note of reminiscence, sharpened to a more rapid utterance—a crescendo for which I had been waiting.

"I haven't an attractive character," he resumed; "I don't want you to think that I have, and so accord me more sympathy than I deserve. Please be quite impartial. Please realise that, according to ordinary standards, I played the part of a cad. Think: there was a man, ostensibly my friend, who had given me the run of his house; I accept his hospitality and his friendship, and then take advantage of his absences to make love to his wife. Not a pretty story, although a commonplace one. Please be quite harsh towards me, and let me be quite harsh towards myself. I did none of the things I ought to have done under the circumstances; I neither went quietly abroad without making a fuss, nor did I attempt to conceal my feelings from her. If you knew her," he said, with an anguish of longing that lit up the whole story for me better than any words of his could have done, "if you knew her, you would realise at once that she wasn't a woman from whom one could conceal one's feelings. There was that calm gentleness about her which made all hypocrisy a shame and a sham. Also, deceiving her would have been like deceiving a child; hurting her was like hurting a child. (That was what enraged me when *he* hurt her, and I had to stand by, and listen.) She was so simple, and direct, and defenceless. So, you see, as soon as I realised what had happened, I told her. It wasn't a dramatic avowal, and it had no very immediately dramatic consequences. In fact, for a while its only effect was to bring me across the room from my habitual arm-chair, to sit on the floor near her with my head against her knee; and so we would remain for hours, not moving, scarcely speaking, for there was such harmony and such content between us that we seemed to know everything that passed in each other's minds."

"Of course, that couldn't last. We were young and human, you see; and standing in the background, overshadowing the perfection of our solitary hours, was his long, sarcastic figure—her husband and my friend. An impossible situation, when you come to consider it. The evenings that he spent at home very soon became intolerable, from every point of view. I grew so nervous with the strain of keeping a hold on myself, that even her tenderness could no longer soothe me. He didn't seem to notice anything amiss, and, you know, the funny, horrible, contradictory part was that, much as I now hated him, I was still conscious of his charm. And so, I think, was she. Can't you picture the trio in that little Chelsea room, while the barges floated by, and she and I sat on opposite sides of the fireplace, so terribly aware of one another, and *he* lay on the sofa, his long legs trailing over the end, discoursing in his admirable and varied way on life, politics, and letters? I wonder in how many London drawing-rooms that situation was being simultaneously reproduced?

"Why do I bore you with a recital so commonplace?" he exclaimed, bringing his fist down on the table; "are you beginning to ask yourself that? What have you to do with journalistic adulteries? Only wait: you shan't complain that the sequel is commonplace, and perhaps, one day, when you read in the papers the sequel to the sequel, you will remember and be entertained. He caught us red-handed, you see. It was one evening when we hadn't expected him home until after midnight, and at ten o'clock the door opened and he stood suddenly in the room. Squalid enough, isn't it? To this day I don't know whether he had laid a trap for us, or whether he was as surprised as we were. He stood there stock still, and I sprang up and stood too, and we glared across at one another. After a moment he said, 'Paolo and Francesca? this scene acquires quite a classic dignity, doesn't it, from frequent repetition?' And then he said the most astonishing thing; he said, 'Don't let me disturb you, and above all remember that *I don't mind*,' and with that he went out of the room and shut the door.

"After that," said the man with the white hair, "I didn't go near the house for a week. This was at her request, and of course I couldn't refuse her. During that week she telephoned to me daily, once in the morning and once in the evening, always with the same story: she had seen nothing of him. He had not even been home to collect any of his clothes. You may imagine the state of anxiety I lived in during that week, which his disappearance did nothing to palliate, but rather heightened by leaving everything so mysterious and uncertain. She was evidently terrified—I could hear it in her voice—but implored me to keep away, for her sake, if not for mine. At the end of the week he appeared without warning in the office of the paper where I worked, and, greeting me without making any allusion to what had happened, invited me to come for two days' sailing in a small boat which had been lent him by a friend.

"I was startled enough by this incongruous suggestion, but naturally I accepted: you couldn't refuse such an invitation from a man who, you suspected, intended to have such a matter out with you on the open sea. We started immediately, and all the way down in the train for Cornwall he talked in his usual manner, undeterred by the fact that I never answered him. We got out at Penzance, the time then being, I suppose, about six o'clock in the evening. I had never been to Penzance before, but he seemed to know his way about, walking me briskly down to the harbour, where a fishing-smack under the charge of a rough-looking sailor was waiting for him. By now I was quite certain that he meant to have it out with me, and for my part, after the long uncertainty of the week, I asked nothing better than to get to grips with him. All I prayed for was a hand-to-hand struggle in which I might have the luck to tip him overboard, so I was rather dismayed when I saw that the sailor was to accompany us.

"We started without any delay, getting clear of the port just as the darkness fell and the first stars came out in a pale green sky. I had never been with him anywhere but in London, and it crossed my mind that it was odd to be with him so far away, off this rocky coast, in the solitude of waters; and I looked at the green sky above the red-brown sails of the fishing-smack, and thought of the barges floating down the river at Chelsea. They were ships, and this was a ship; they carried men, and this one also carried men. I looked at my companion, who sat in the stern holding the tiller. There was a breeze, which drove us along at quite a smart pace. 'Cornwall,' I said to myself, staring slowly round the bay and at the black mass of St. Michael's Mount, Cornwall. . .''

"I don't know how many hours we sailed that night, but I know that when the day broke we were out of sight of land. All that while we had not spoken a word, though to all practical purposes we were alone, the sailor having gone to sleep for'ard on a heap of nets, in the bottom of the boat. He was a rough, handsome, foreign-looking fellow, of a type I believe often to be found in that part of England. I couldn't understand the object of this sailing expedition at all. It seemed to me an unnecessarily elaborate introduction to the discussion of a subject which could as well have been thrashed out in London. Still, as the other man was the aggrieved party, I supposed that he was entitled to the choice of weapons; I supposed that his devilish sense of humour was at the bottom of all this, and I was determined not to give him the chance of saying I wouldn't play up. But why couldn't he tell me what was in his mind? How far did he mean to take me out to sea first? These questions and others raced through my mind during the whole of that night, while I sat back leaning against the sides of the boat, watching the stars pass overhead and listening to the gentle sip, sip of the water.

"At dawn my companion rose, and, shading his eyes with one hand while with the other he still held the tiller, he stood up scanning the surface of the waters. I watched him, resolved that it would not be me who spoke first. After a while he appeared to find what he was looking for, for he said, 'Nearly there.' I could see nothing to break the whole pale opal stretch of sunrise-flushing sea but a small black speck which I took to be a buoy, and the faint echo of its bell was borne to me through the clear air. He sat down again beside the tiller, and we sailed on in the same silence, into the loveliness of the morning. I was quite certain that he had some sinister purpose, though what it was I could not yet imagine. What did he mean by that 'Nearly there'? Although he did not actually stir, he gave me the impression of concentration now, and at a word from him the sailor awoke and shot a rapid glance at me, as though doubtful whether he would find me still in the boat. I was beginning to wonder whether I should be a match for the two of them, when my companion, leaving the tiller, made a step towards me with a handkerchief he had drawn from his pocket; the sailor pinioned my arms from behind, and no sooner had I recognised the peculiar smell of chloroform than I was insensible and inert between them.

"It was very neatly done. I might have trusted him to carry out neatly whatever he undertook. Even over that he compelled my angry admiration. So neat! the fiend, the devil, he had got the better of me before I had had the chance to put up even the feeblest struggle. I curse myself now for my silly bravado in accompanying him when he asked me. I might have known I wasn't a match for him. But I'll be even with him yet," he said, his nervous hands fumbling at his collar, "I'll be even with him yet; I'll bide my time," and never was vindictiveness more savage in human eyes.

"He didn't allow me to come to my senses until he had carried out his purpose. When I opened my eyes I was *inside* the cage of the buoy, with the bell swinging gently to and fro above my head.

"Have you ever seen one of those buoys? They consist of a pear-shaped iron cage fixed on to a sort of platform, like the keel of a dinghy, and the bell hangs between four clappers at the top of the cage, and as the thing rocks up and down on the swell of the sea the clappers hit against the bell. There was just room for me to sit on the platform, crouched up inside the cage. One section of the cage was hinged to open, and the door thus formed was secured by a padlock; how he had got the key of it Heaven alone knows. I have tried to convey to you—haven't I?—that he was a very able and successful fellow.

"When I came to, he was circling slowly round and round the buoy in his sailing-boat, lounging indifferently beside the tiller, and watching me with an expression of mockery I can't reproduce in words. I lost my head then; I leapt up and shook the bars of my cage and screamed to him to let me out. I can hear now in my ears the futility of my own voice screaming across the placid emptiness of the water. I must have looked like a trapped ape—the kind of ape that is most like a man. I shook the iron bars so violently that the whole of my floating prison jumped about, and the bell began to ring loudly. He only lounged and smiled. No doubt he had looked forward extremely to the moment. His amused impassivity was the thing best calculated to restore my self-control, and I try to salve my vanity by thinking that I should never so have gratified him but for the bewildering effects of the anaesthetic. I calmed myself down, I tried to reason with him.

"I exhorted him to settle up his wrongs in a more civilised manner. Then, seeing that every plea was to him a source of fresh delight, I ceased to argue, and became silent, holding on to the bars of my cage and watching him as he cruised slowly round and round the buoy. Presently he talked to me. They were like neat incisions in my flesh, his words. Oh, he spared me nothing, I assure you; there wasn't a phrase without a beautifully tempered edge to it. I recalled his words when he had caught us together, "Don't let me disturb you, and above all remember that '*I don't mind*,'" and even in the midst of my rage and hatred I couldn't help respecting him for that irony.

"I learnt now the full extent to which he had minded. Quite coldly he told me. He had spent the week wondering whether it should be himself or me that should be put out of the way. So much had he minded, you see. I think he had been hurt in his pride, even more than in his affection for. . . for her. I hadn't suspected that he was so sensitive over what he considered his honour—dense of me, perhaps—but there was no mistaking that this sensitiveness now tied the extra lash on to the whip of his tongue. When he had finished talking, when he had said all that he wanted to say, and all without once losing his temper or his damned insolent dexterity, he nodded to me for all the world as though we had been talking shop in Fleet Street, and were separating to go about our various businesses. That nod remains with me; I'll never forget it or forgive it; it seemed to me the last crowning insult; it seemed to sum up all that I most hated in the man.

"He put his boat about, she heeled over a little as the breeze took her, and that slight slant of her sail was pencilled against the pale sky as she glided away across the water. I can't resist the journalistic touch, you see," he added, with an outburst of extraordinary bitterness.

"It was not until his boat had dwindled to a tiny black dot far away that I began fully to realise the situation. There was I, alone in the middle of a great circle of sea and sky, alone and confined, and ludicrously helpless. At first it was upon the ludicrous aspect that I chiefly dwelt, the anger of it, the absurdity, and the humiliation. Then little by little the horror of it crept over me, and I was aghast; there was, of course, the gleam of hope that I might attract the attention of a passing ship, but the Channel at that point must be fairly on the way to becoming the Atlantic, and I dared not delude myself too boldly lest I be disappointed. He wasn't coming back for me; he had made that quite clear. He had left beside me on the bottom of the buoy a parcel of food and a bottle of water, enough, he had said, to keep me for a week if I used it sparingly. He had said, with a grin, that I would be all right for a week if the weather kept calm. If not, he was afraid I might be inconvenienced. But he would like me to have a week, because that was exactly the length of time that he had had. Those had been his last words before he nodded and said, 'So long.'

"The whole of that day passed in a dead calm. I sat on the floor with my arms clasped round my knees, because there wasn't room to stretch out my legs, and when I became too cramped in that position I stood up, which I could just manage to do if I stooped my head. Later on I found out that I could stand upright by putting my head inside the bell, but I couldn't bear that for very long because of the intolerable noise of the clappers hitting the bell so near my ears. I tried holding the clappers still, but that was no good, as there were four of them. So I held the bell itself, which at least deadened the sound. No, I couldn't unhook the clappers; they were a fixture. Anyhow, that first day I wasn't much troubled by the noise of the bell, as the buoy rocked very slightly on an oily swell; I was more troubled by the dazzle of the sun on the water, not daring to shut my eyes for long lest I should miss a possible ship, and also I was divided between the gnawing of my thoughts and the boredom of those interminable hours from sunrise to sunset. I don't suppose it is given to many men to have nothing better to do than watch the sun travel across the heavens from the moment it emerges above one horizon to the moment it dips below the rim of the other. That was what I watched—the delicacy of dawn, the blood-red of sunset, and the grand golden sweep of the journey in between the two.

"Never had I felt so abandoned or so insignificant. Can your imagination enter into it at all? To do so, you must keep the sense of the enormous circle of sea always present in your mind, the hard round edge of the horizon, and the buoy in the centre like a speck of dust in the centre of a plate. I felt I was in a tiny prison in the middle of an enormous prison. And after the sun had gone it was worse; it is true that I could no longer see that huge hard circle, but I knew that, although invisible, it was still there, and now in addition I had a black vault over me, and it grew cold, and a loneliness closed down on me such as I had not experienced while I had the sun and his warmth for companions. I dared not contemplate the prospect of many such days and nights; I simply dared not let myself think. I tried to sleep, but was too cold. A breeze sprang up at about midnight, and the buoy rocked more noticeably; again, I dared not picture my discomfort should the weather change. I called it discomfort; I didn't know then, I hadn't yet begun to learn.

"Two days passed like that. Two whole days. Have you ever tried to spend two days, or even one day, or even twelve hours, doing absolutely and literally nothing? If not, try it, especially if you happen to be an active man. I could only sit there, my knees drawn up and my hands either clasped round my knees or hanging between them. I was confronted all the time by the thought of what the end was to be. Starvation and death from thirst? I could see very little other prospect. For the first day I had been comparatively sanguine that a ship would come along, but hourly this hope dwindled, till there was no real hope left, but only the old obscure and unreasoning human obstinacy. So on the second day I suffered from my thoughts; I hadn't, as yet, undergone any real physical suffering.

"The morning of the third day broke with dark clouds over a grey sea. It was indescribably dreary. All that water, all that mass of grey water! I huddled my knees up against my chest for warmth. A shower fell, and I minded that because it meant more water, not only because it chilled me; don't think I exaggerate: the quantity and the monotony of so much water was getting on my nerves. They were in a pretty bad state by then, so bad that the dread of ultimate madness had already crossed my mind. I was weakened, too, by insufficient food, for I knew I must economise my resources. Once or twice steamers passed, a very long way off. I shouted till my throat was hoarse, but quite in vain. Each time they passed out of sight, I sobbed. Forgive me.

"The wind held, driving the masses of low clouds across the sky, and chopping the sea into little waves, white-topped amongst the grey, which tumbled and tossed the buoy till I was sickened and wearied. I fancied that the pulp of my brain was being shaken to and fro inside my head; it felt like that. I prayed for the wind to go down, but it only gained in strength. I felt I should go mad; I was so impotent, you see. And the bell clanged above my head—I was condemned to unceasing movement and unceasing noise."

He stared round him with tormented eyes, as though afraid that the whole restaurant would begin rocking and vibrating.

"And there were other things, ridiculous and humiliating," he resumed, "that robbed me even of the small consolation of tragedy. How can I tell you? I shall lose all dignity in your eyes—if indeed I ever had any to lose—as I lost it in my own. The terrible sickness, you understand. . . That, and the din of the bell, and being flung up and down, backwards and forwards. No rest, not for a moment. I prayed, I tried to fight my way out of the buoy, between the bars, to throw myself into the sea. The sea was rising visibly, and the spray of the waves broke over me, drenching me; the salt dried upon my face, stiffening my skin.

There were moments when I thought I could endure the rest, if I might have a respite from the movement; other moments, if I might have a respite from the sickness; and yet others, if I might have a respite from the clang of the bell. In the intervals of the sickness, with such strength as remained to me, I tore strips from my soaking shirt and tried to bind up the clappers; it muffled the noise a little, but not much. I wept from weariness and despair.

"It pursues me," he said, again putting his head between his hands and shaking it with the same tired mournfulness; "at nights I think that my bed is flung up and down, and when I spring out the room reels round me as though I were drunk. There was no escape. It was no use trying to bend the bars of the cage, or to pull up the planks of the bottom. And the sickness, the sickness! It tore me, it shattered me, but never for a moment did I lose consciousness of the supreme humiliation it brought on me, and I supposed that he had foreseen this; surely he had foreseen every detail. Secure in London, by now, he was surely rubbing his hands together as he thought of the derelict ceaselessly tossing up and down at sea." He gave a kind of snarl. "I pictured him, as no doubt he was picturing me."

"The real storm came next day, and I had to cling to the bars of the cage with both hands to save myself from being flung from side to side and broken against the iron. There were periods, I think, when I fainted from exhaustion, emerging incredibly bruised, and instantly in the grip of the sickness again. The buoy was hurled about, down into the grey valleys between the waves, drenched over and over with masses of water, as though some giant were flinging down enormous pailfuls; indeed, it remains a mystery to me why I wasn't drowned. No doubt I would have been if the light platform hadn't floated like a cork. The bell was ringing wildly all the time. Everytime I went down with the buoy I saw the sky tilting impossibly over my head, and the wave curling up above me before it smashed and fell, burying me beneath it."

He became silent, and sat for a long while heavily brooding to himself. Once or twice he closed his eyes, as though his thoughts were causing him intolerable pain. I knew that he was living again through all that racket and nightmare. I didn't say anything; the thunder of the storm roared too loudly in my head for me to upraise my small voice against it, or to offer my tiny sympathy to that man whose endurance had been measured against the elements, and whose standard must be forever after raised to the summit of their standard.

He let fall one or two phrases that seemed to open a rift down into the mirk of his experience, so that I thought I looked for a moment into the very night that he described:

"I had simply given up hope. I was so weak, you understand. By the time that night came I was just letting myself be thrown about, anyhow, quite limp, my head rolling and my arms flacking; I must have looked like a man in a fit. Whenever I opened my eyes I saw the moon between the clouds rushing furiously down the sky, and rushing back the other way as another wave took me up again on its crest. The light of the moon was just sufficient to light up the rough and tumble of the inky hills of water. I remember thinking quite stupidly to myself that the moon was a dead world, and that I envied her for being dead. All this happened to me," he said, frowning across the table with sudden intentness, "the week before last."

This mention of human time brought me back with a shock from the fantastic world to which he had transported me.

"Hallo!" I said, starting as one awakened, and making in my confusion a ridiculous remark, "it must be getting very late."

Only the ceiling light burnt in the little restaurant, which but for ourselves was deserted. The stranger leant over towards me, and a shiver passed over me at the nearness of this man whom I did not know, and to whose extraordinary experience I had, so to speak, by my own doing, been made a party. I wanted to put an end to it now, I wanted to say, "Yes, I have been very much interested. Thank you very much for telling me," and then to get up and go away. But at my first movement he detained me.

"Listen a little longer. I'm not mad, you know, and you needn't be afraid that I shall ever bother you afterwards. You don't know what good this has done me. I've been alone with this thing for a fortnight, nearly, thinking about it. The storm. . . It lasted for two days; that made four days since I had been on the buoy. I think another day of storm would have killed me, there wasn't much life left in me by the time the sea began to go down. Two days of storm. . ."

His voice trailed away. I think he felt, as I did, that the moment was over when he had really held all my attention and all my imagination. It was no good trying to revive it. I was tired, as though I had lived through some brief but violent mental stress.

"Two days of storm," he muttered vaguely.

"And how did you get away?" I asked; it was a perfunctory question.

"How did I get away.—Oh.—Yes, of course. A ship, on the seventh day. Yes, there were three days of calm after the storm; comparative calm, but for the swell. So I had the week he had intended for me to have, to the full. The ship's carpenter came alongside in a dinghy, and filed through one of the bars. I never told them how I came to be there. I said it was for a bet, and that I was to have been fetched by my friends the next day. When I got on board I collapsed. I'd just come out of hospital the day you first saw me here." He rose wearily. "Well, I mustn't keep you. Thank you more than I can say, for having listened."

It seemed strange that *he* should be thanking *me*.

We walked towards the door of the restaurant together; outside, the London street was empty under a melancholy drizzle of rain.

"You had better give me your name and your address," I said, pricked on to it by a curiously conventional conscience.

"No, no," he said, backing away from me. "You've been kind, you mustn't ever be implicated."

"Why, what are you going to do?" I cried.

He turned, his old wideawake crammed down over his hair, and his face half buried in the upturned collar of his coat, but I saw the sudden gleam of his eyes by the light of a street lamp.

"Think out something worse to do to him," he mumbled rapidly; "something worse to do to *him*."

As HE READ THE LAST words M. Lesueur's brow darkened. A mare's nest indeed! An hour gone and nothing gained! Then his eye caught a footnote to the last page of the translation he had just perused.

"About the middle of this story" (the footnote said) "I found a few words in brackets that seem to have no connection with the tale. They are in French—foreigner's French and faulty—but they appear to mean: 'We are imprisoned in the garret under the leads of the long wing of the château. Our food will last only another day.'" This laconic footnote was initialled "H. F. (translator)."

The Commissary's eye brightened. Here at last was something, and something good. Rapidly he made his plans. He would start in twenty minutes with six men; he would advise Toussaint by telephone to meet him at the château with six more. The case would prove, perhaps, vastly important. He saw decorations and Paris employment; he read in imagination columns of praise in the great papers of the capital. Quitting unwillingly the realm of ambitious fancy, he took up the telephone, but before he could speak there came a sharp knock at the door, and a gendarme stood awaiting permission to address his superior.

"What is it?" demanded M. Lesueur.

"A tramp, sir," replied the gendarme.

"God in heaven, man! What do I care for a tramp? Is this a workhouse? Send him away and go after him!"

"He has found two Englishmen in a dungeon," observed the gendarme with wooden persistence.

"Let him join them!" snapped M. Lesueur, angrily. Then the next moment, "What do you say? Englishmen? Where? What dungeon?"

"He asks leave to make his deposition, sir. He is not an ordinary tramp."

For a moment the commissary hesitated. The memory of those words interpolated in the third of the mysterious stories checked his impatience. Never neglect possible information.

"Bring him in," he said shortly, and replaced the telephone receiver that, all this while and to the intense irritation of the exchange, he had held vaguely in his hand.

There was ushered in a lean, scarecrow figure at whose heels (despite scuffling protests from the gendarme without) limped a black, untidy dog. The tramp bowed and began at once to speak in the slow correct French of a well-educated foreigner. He told of a dusty road along which he had toiled; of a coppice and its tempting shade; of the drowsiness of afternoon; of dream voices that were not, after all, of dream; of a mound with a mysterious grating; of a subterranean cavern and its two unusual and impatient prisoners. M. Lesueur listened in silence. The story done, he took up the telephone once again. While waiting for his connection, he addressed the senior gendarme of those present in the room.

"I want the two fastest cars brought round immediately. This fellow shall take us to his mound and we will see how far he is lying and how far telling us the truth. We will then proceed to the Château de la Hourmerie. Six men will be required to accompany me. Make your selection—'allô! 'allô!— Toussaint?— Is that you, Toussaint?"

And he outlined with curt efficiency the instructions laid down for his subordinate.

"In an hour," he concluded, "we meet at the Château de la Hourmerie. One hour, mind you! One hour from now." Smartly and with finality he hung up the receiver.

The Commissary was already struggling into his dust coat when there came yet a second interruption. The sound of many agitated feet in the outer office prepared the occupants of M. Lesueur's private room for threatened but not for actual invasion of their retired sanctuary. Wherefore they regarded with speechless amazement the tempestuous entry of two elegantly gowned women, one clutching the other firmly by the arm, while in close and uncomfortable attendance followed two men, one tall, white-whiskered, and conspicuous in a buff alpaca suit, the other short, stout, and shining with the sweat-drops of embarrassment.

The female invaders lost no time in stating their business, but as they both spoke at once and shrilly, the unfortunate Commissary learnt little of the matter at issue between them. Not until the united efforts of all the men present had silenced feminine vociferation was it possible to understand what in the world the pother was about. The old gentleman, to whom in courtesy priority of speech was accorded, made the following statement:

"About an hour and a half ago I entered the Casino in company with the young lady whom now you observe in the grip of—er—the other lady. My companion, whose name is Amélie, was anxious at once to join the crowd at the tables.

"We contrived to edge ourselves to a convenient front seat, and for some while played quietly and with varying success. I then observed that new-comers were seeking to force a way to the front row of players, and, in order to give others their turn, stepped behind my companion, leaving vacant the spot I had previously occupied. It was filled forthwith by the second of the two ladies now before you, who thanked me with a charming smile for my courtesy, and was on the point of turning her interest wholly to the game when her eyes fell on Amélie. Instantly she flushed with excitement, paled again and flushed once more, and I was the next moment aware of a rapid movement of her arm as she snatched from the neck of Amélie an ornament that hung there from a thin gold chain.

"You can imagine the excited confusion that ensued, the outcome of which is my attendance here to account, so far as I may, for the disturbance in which I have been involved."

M. Lesueur acknowledged die straightforward simplicity of the old gentleman's story with a slight bow.

"Your name, sir?" he asked.

"Widiershaw. I am an Englishman."

"Did you know any of these persons before this afternoon?"

"Yes and no. Yes—because the lady who assaulted Amélie in the Casino turns out to be the widow of a relative of mine, and her name, although not her person, is quite familiar to me. No—because my acquaintance with Mdlle Amélie predated by an hour only our visit to the Casino. This gentleman I have never seen before."

The Commissary suddenly recalled his waiting motor-cars, his telephoned appointment, his sensational prospects at the Château de la Hourmerie. Between him and the door of his room was an excited and perspiring crowd, not the least awesome members of which were the two angry ladies. By ill-luck his second in command was ill and away from work. Next in seniority came an official, competent enough to deal with ordinary cases of theft, disturbance, or general misdemeanour, but hardly to be trusted with an affair deserving of delicate and cautious management. M. Lesueur felt obscurely that the present was an affair of that kind. The parties to it were not only well dressed, but (with the possible exception of Amélie, whose social complacency the evidence of Mr. Withershaw appeared to have established) suggestive of good breeding, or at least of normal good behaviour. It would not do, thanks to the inexperience of a subordinate, to involve the Commissariat of St. Hilaire in unpleasantness with foreigners of influence and distinction.

With a sigh of impatience M. Lesueur turned again to his chair and sat down. He gave an order to the gendarme at his elbow:

"Telephone Toussaint that I am delayed, that I will be at La Hourmerie half an hour later than I said. Perhaps forty minutes. The cars can wait."

He spoke in a low voice, but not so low that the quick ear of Amélie did not catch the words "La Hourmerie." She compressed her lips, cast a look of spiteful triumph at her antagonist (who still held her arm as in a vice), and awaited developments in vengeful silence.

"Now!" said the Commissary briskly. "Your names, please. M. Withershaw—prénom? Thank you. M. *James* Withershaw. Yours, madame? Pardon? Spell it, please."

"D-A-N-E—trait d'union—V-E-R-E-K-E-R," said the captor lady, with precision and a very passable accent.

"Amélie Vildrac."

"Hector Turpin."

A clerk made the necessary entries. Mrs. Dane-Vereker was asked to give her version of the afternoon's events.

"They are few and easy to relate," she said. "This woman was my maid. Two days ago she stole, among other things, a valuable and valued cameo belonging to me, and disappeared. This afternoon, and by the merest hazard, I found myself next to her at the tables. With an effrontery natural to women of her type she was wearing the very ornament she had stolen. Naturally I charged her with the theft, and attempted to seize my property. That is all I have to say."

"And you, Mdlle Vildrac?"

Amélie shrugged insolent shoulders.

"Things have an air so different from different points of view," she observed. "Madame tells her story. I tell mine. Which will you believe? Here are the real facts. It is true, as Madame has said, that until two days ago I was Madame's maid. It is also true in effect that two days ago I left her. But not clandestinely, oh no! nor with stolen valuables. Rather at her bidding, and with a small trinket that she gave to me at parting. 'Amélie,' she said to me, 'I have planned to leave these people we are with'—you must understand, Monsieur, that Madame and I were members of a touring party under the charge of M. Hector Turpin yonder. Mon Dieu, how strange some of that party! English, all of them, and so strange!— But I was saying that Madame had planned to leave them. 'I am going away with M. Turpin,' she said to me, 'and these stupid people must extricate themselves as best they may from the trap into which my clever Turpin has led them. You will not betray me? Go you to Paris or to St. Hilaire and seek your fortune. Here is money and here is the cameo you have so often admired. Wear it in memory of me, and for its sake keep silence.'"

"Voila!" Mdlle Amélie spread out emphatic hands. "Am I a thief? Is it theft to take gifts from another woman? And finally, M. le Commissaire, seeing that you are bound for La Hourmerie, I ask you to observe that this precious elopement took place from that very spot, and that in the Château de la Hourmerie were staying those other unfortunates, now abandoned to their fate by the selfish passion of Madame for her cicerone turned paramour!"

It may be imagined that Amélie's scandalous declaration let loose Babel once again in the office of the unhappy Commissary. Mrs. Dane-Vereker, Turpin, Amélie, and Mr. Withershaw vociferated simultaneously and with prolonged fervour. The patience of M. Lesueur came finally to an end.

"Silence!" he roared, banging the desk in frenzy. And then to the attendant gendarmes, who, by now, numbered some twelve highly edified stalwarts, he shouted an order for the instant incarceration of these pestilent folk. Their fate should be decided on the morrow.

"As for you, Mademoiselle," he said to Amélie, "I know your type well, and I ask you to note that I am indeed bound for La Hourmerie. I shall not forget your story. Between this moment and tomorrow you will have time to think of the various embellishments of which it is susceptible."

And he hurried from the room toward the outer door, followed by six gendarmes, and, between two of them, the tramp, while from the office they had left came a confused turmoil of bitter feminine insult, of French official determination, of furious Anglo-Saxon protest. Baba, the black dog, bundled in his master's wake.

On the terrace of the Château de la Hourmerie clustered a motley and excited group. In the centre M. Lesueur, his face alight with the satisfaction of a quest worthily fulfilled, gazed almost fondly at the body of rescuers and rescued that bore witness to his triumph. First was the tramp, impassive as ever, his whole bearing a slouch of uninterested fatigue. By his side—unshaven, a little dusty, but otherwise no whit the worse—stood the Professor and the Bureaucrat, salved from their underground prison by the crowbars of the six muscular policemen who formed at the present impressive juncture a stolid back-drop to the scene. Close by, also unshaven and weary-looking, but happy in the moment of release, were a priest, a poet, and a nondescript young man of amiable aspect and engaging mien, whose name was Peter Brown. M. Lesueur had just completed his narrative of events at the Commissariat of Police.

"Good Lord!" said the Bureaucrat. "Fancy Mrs. Dane bolting with old Turps!"

"I shall never write another story on wallpaper," remarked Peter Brown. "It's worse than marking handkerchiefs. But we could make no one hear, and thought, if we hurled out of the window a bundle of paper with a message hidden somewhere in the middle of apparently harmless text, there was just a chance of its being picked up. The lane runs fairly near to yonder corner of the house. You can imagine how thrilled we were when the old envelope—weighted with Father Anthony's pocket knife and my pipe stop—fell plump into a passing cart."

"The chance was indeed providential," commented the Priest gravely, "but let us not forget that we owe to our zealous and sharp-eyed friends among the police the actual discovery of our queer message hidden in the grass of the crossroads."

"Where are the others of the party?" broke in the Bureaucrat. "We know that Turpin and Mrs. Dane and that minx Amélie are in jail. But where are Miss Pogson and Doctor Pennock and Mr. Scott, and where's old what's-his-name, the Master Printer? . . ."

THE REPLY WAS UNEXPECTED. SOMEWHERE at the back of the château a clock struck noisily. In their basket chairs on the terrace of the Château de la Hourmerie the members of Mr. Hector Turpin's first Continental touring party sat spellbound at the force of a chime hitherto unnoticed. They had counted twelve strokes. To their horrified amazement, the chime rang out once more—and they realised that the tall windows of the house no longer threw comforting light upon the flagstones, that behind them, as before, lay utter darkness.

Seven voices spoke as one:

"Did you hear it? The clock struck thirteen!"

And again:

"Did you see, the way the lights went out?"

For a moment there was profound silence. Then from the last chair of the line came a long-drawn, chuckling laugh, a laugh of pride, of amusement, of relief,

"Well, upon my word!" said in quiet, incisive tones the voice of Henry Scott (of the Psychical Research Society). "I hardly dared to hope for so complete a triumph! My good friends, it is one A.M. As the clock struck twelve you sank into hypnotic trance; on the point of its striking one, you emerged. The hour of interval was telescoped in your waking consciousness to a few seconds. As for the lights—at half-past twelve Doctor Pennock went to bed. She turned them out as she passed through the house. I asked her to. I will relight them now."

And he walked to the nearest window, crossed the room within and switched on every lamp.

The bemused wits of the victims of Mr. Scott's hypnotic joke could not immediately respond to this sudden revelation of the truth. Also their eyes blinked in the new brilliance of projected light. Mrs. Dane-Vereker was the first to recover speech.

"But where is that wretch Amélie?" she gasped.

"And the Commissary?" demanded Father Anthony.

"And the Old Gentleman?" echoed the Courier.

"Turpin, by the lord Harry!" shouted the Bureaucrat. "But you've eloped with Mrs. Dane!"

"The guile of an enemy detained me in a damp and poorly ventilated cave," complained the Professor.

"There was a tramp here with a dog!" moaned the poet.

"The terrace was crowded with police!" cried Peter Brown, "and it was still daylight! . . ."

Mr. Scott enjoyed their bewilderment with the cruel calm of the true psychological investigator.

"You will never see any of those people again," he observed quietly. "Except poor Amélie, who is in bed this three hours, I invented them all. Not a bad set of creations, were they?"

A snore from the shadow drew attention to the stertorous oblivion of Mr. Buck, the retired master printer.

"Buck was my only failure," said the psychical researcher. "He was fast asleep when I started in. I say nothing of Doctor Pennock; she was too much for me; but then she knows the game. Nevertheless, she had the sportsmanship to leave me at it."

By this time signs of considerable indignation were visible among the dupes of Mr. Scott's inventive skill. The Lady of Fashion recalled with blushing fury her supposed escapade with the absurd Courier. The Bureaucrat re-lived his angry helplessness behind the iron grille. Before, however, anger could break out, the tension gave way to the irrepressible humour of Peter Brown. Suddenly he began to laugh, and each moment he laughed more loudly and more shamelessly. One by one the others joined, until by the healthy wind of merriment every trailing wisp of irritation was dispelled and blown away. Mr. Scott rose to his feet.

"You are admirable folk," he said, "the whole collection of you! I am proud to be associated with so unselfish and humorous an assembly. Let me make some slight amends for my impertinence. In the first place, I would ask your pardon for subjecting you without warning or permission to a most interesting experiment. In the second place, let me tell you a tale against myself, a tale that shows me in the light of a bewildered, blundering fool. I had never, until the complete success of the unwarrantable trick I have just played upon you excellent people, really recovered from the depression of this adventure. It will discipline my vanity to tell the story, for I can hardly think of it without nervousness. Surely, by the time it has been made verbally public, I shall be chastened as befits simple humanity."

A Note About the Author

V. Sackville-West (1892–1952) was an English novelist, poet, journalist, and gardener. Born at Knole, the Sackville's hereditary home in west Kent, Vita was the daughter of English peer Lionel Sackville-West and his cousin Victoria, herself the illegitimate daughter of the 2nd Baron Sackville and a Spanish dancer named Pepita. Educated by governesses as a young girl, Vita later attended school in Mayfair, where she met her future lover Violet Keppel. An only child, she entertained herself by writing novels, plays, and poems in her youth, both in English and French. At the age of eighteen, she made her debut in English society and was courted by powerful and well-connected men. She had affairs with men and women throughout her life, leading an open marriage with diplomat Harold Nicholson. Following their wedding in 1913, the couple moved to Constantinople for one year before returning to settle in England, where they raised two sons. Vita's most productive period of literary output, in which she published such works as *The Land* (1926) and *All Passion Spent* (1931), coincided with her affair with English novelist Virginia Woolf, which lasted from 1925 to 1935. The success of Vita's writing—published through Woolf's Hogarth Press—allowed her lover to publish some of her masterpieces, including *The Waves* (1931) and *Orlando* (1928), the latter being inspired by Sackville-West's family history, androgynous features, and unique personality. Vita died at the age of seventy at Sissinghurst Castle, where she worked with her husband to design one of England's most famous gardens.

A Note from the Publisher

Spanning many genres, from non-fiction essays to literature classics to children's books and lyric poetry, Mint Edition books showcase the master works of our time in a modern new package. The text is freshly typeset, is clean and easy to read, and features a new note about the author in each volume. Many books also include exclusive new introductory material. Every book boasts a striking new cover, which makes it as appropriate for collecting as it is for gift giving. Mint Edition books are only printed when a reader orders them, so natural resources are not wasted. We're proud that our books are never manufactured in exce
quantity they need to be read and enjoyed.

Discover more of your favorite classics with Bookfinity™.

- Track your reading with custom book lists.
- Get great book recommendations for your personalized Reader Type.
- Add reviews for your favorite books.
- AND MUCH MORE!

Visit **bookfinity.com** and take the fun Reader Type quiz to get started.

Enjoy our classic and modern companion pairings!